The Splintered Eye

A collection of contemporary horror, science fiction and dark fantasy by Alien Rabbit.

Contributing Writers

Donny Gray

Walter Smitty

Stan Mikhailov

Christopher Godber

Simon Ross

Polina Chistyakova

The Three eyes are as follows

(!) Dark Eye (Fantasy Horror / Dark Comedy)

<[**]> Journeys through The Dark (Gothic Horror / Thriller / Psychological Horror)

[(::)] Warpgate (Science Fiction / Fantasy / Occult Fantasy)

Artworks generated with Leonardo.ai*
***(No public artworks were used for the artworks)**

Editor: Christopher Godber

The Splintered Eye

A Dark Fantasy Collection for Halloween 2023

Alien Rabbit Limited

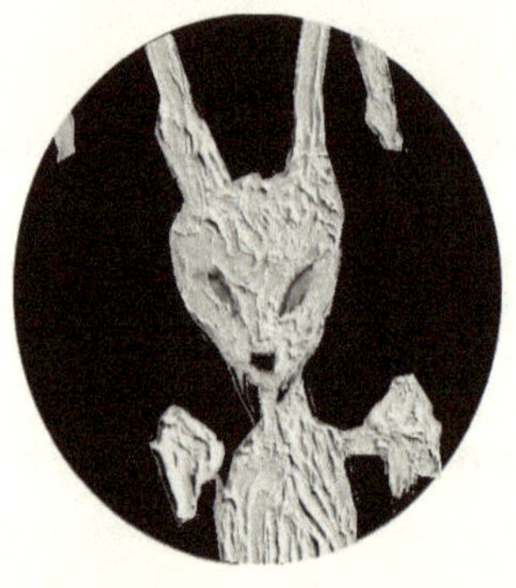

Alien Rabbit Limited

ISBN: 978-1-7391474-8-8

www.alienrabbit.co.uk

"There is no exquisite beauty... without some strangeness in the proportion."

— Edgar Allan Poe

CONTENTS [:]

Dark Eye (!)

"Evil has only the power that we give it." — Ray Bradbury,

Lesson of the Pale One by Chris Godber

The pale one looked down onto his circular table, adorned with a variety of arcane sigils and symbols pulsating with a red glow in a dark room, lit only by dim candlelights. They were all arranged in a spiral pattern like a vortex turning in on itself. He was tall and thin as if he was some gnarled old tree in a dying forest, bald with a large lightning strike scar marked across his face with eyes that would seem to stare intensely into one's soul, mad staring eyes that had seen horror, terror and strife and a face that was half bushy white beard. His thin fingers pointed at the sigil to the left of the spiral and he began to recite his arcane incantation;

"Bim Dazza Noga Dim, Dom Dom Dom de bazza Boo, Alla MackdooBazzaDe"

And with a flick of his hand the spell was cast, and a bright blue flash of energy exploded from the symbol before him, it was an inverted cross! And from the depths the dim form of a figure began to appear before the dark sorcerer, who could already feel the presence of the archaic arcana in the room.

"Mashagga de logga me logga" a croaking demonic tone spoke from the shadows "alaka shabba laka" as the sorcerer noticed two softly red glowing eyes glimmering in the darkness

"I, I don't understand" the sorcerer croaked "are you able to speak Romani?"
"I have summoned you Baphomet, to bring us all back to our basic natures, I want the world to return to the Goat! To you my lord! Away from the feeble sheep of Christ!"
"Ahhh I see" the eyes blinked in and out in the darkness as the deep bellowing voice of Baphomet spoke to his servant "And how will we rid this world of the pale imitators of Christ?" he intoned in a questioning, assertive tone, as the sorcerer strained his eyes to see his master's form.

"Spells alone will not suffice, we need sacrifice"
"I understand, master, and what will you have me sacrifice?"
"Yourself"
The pale one cowered and fell backwards a little tripping over a large tome he had left on the floor of his tower, collapsing on his back,
"No, please master! No, anyone but me!"
"Yes" smiled the beast in a sinister manner as it emerged from the shadows to show his true form, as the pale one screamed, his eyes

searching desperately for the door to escape as Bapomet emerged into the light; He was roughly 7ft tall and his hooves made a clacking noise on the wooden floor as the pale one crawled around trying to avert his red glowing gaze as the goat's eyes scanned for him in the darkness. Clack clack went his hooves as the sorcerer desperately searched for a way to escape the beast he had bought into this world.

"Learn the way of the dark one" the goat uttered with a deep tone "and meet our dark lord, in hell"

"I will make it swift necromancer, do not be afraid, you knew forewell were you to play with such powers what the price could be."

And as he said the final words he saw the corner of a red tunic hiding underneath a wooden table and he quickly stamped his hooves down crushing the necromancer's skull, as the sorcerer's head exploded like a watermelon, his brains oozing out of his eyes.

The goat chuckled to itself in the dimly lit study and sat down amongst the tomes of the magical one. "Time to have some fun" his goatface grinned and grabbing a piece of brain from the skull of the necromancer's dead body he performed a transfiguration spell, and became the necromancer incarnate.

The demon now had acquired the form of the pale one himself and he descended down the tower, to see what he could do with his temporary power, to corrupt and kill, to inject a little chaos into wherever he found himself again.

'What a strange sky there is in this place' thought the demon as he looked out the windows, descending down the tower's spiral staircase. The sky was a toxic green and the world's surface was barren and half dead, as if the world was in ruin from some manner of apocalypse.

"This reminds me of home" thought the demon as he entered the bottom of the stairs, at the ground level of the tower, which was made of old bricks. He pushed through the cobwebs and debris which surrounded him to move towards the door on the other side of the basement, and pushed it, it was rather stiff and would not budge so he merely uttered a spell to increase his strength and smashed the door open.

The green polluted air greeted him as the demon looked out at the decaying forest he found himself in, a tower surrounded by marshlands and far from any form of civilised life. He had been summoned to many types of worlds and times and places before, so this was nothing too out of the ordinary for him, but the environment was certainly unnerving, though for a demon like him who was possessed of such supernatural powers, very little to worry about in the long run.

'I must find another sacrifice' he thought 'almost certainly a virgin if possible, as it will sate the tastes of the dark lord'. The Goat walked on and on for several miles before he came before a sign which pointed to any sign of civilisation - it said

Welcome to Transilvanyia, Romania
West - Count Dracul residence
East - Carpathian Mountains

"Ahh a Count, that would be an exquisite aristocratic sacrifice for the Dark Lord" the goat thought, smiling. 'That will indeed please him' and so the demon went west traveling through the mountainous ranges that surrounded him in the dark, under the hue of a full moon, and a poisonous, polluted green sky which heralded death and despair, and as he was about to find out, an evil that equalled his own.

Baphomet approached the castle that stood high before him, large spires reached to the skies above as crows cawed in the distance. He approached the large wooden door before him and rang the bell to the right and waited. He would have to be careful so as not to elicit suspicion of his true nature, and so he performed a quick spell of illusive protection, a spell which blocked people of a perceptive nature picking up on any magical illusions.

A tall thin man dressed in a grand red robe answered the door, he was paler than the pale one who had summoned Baphomet and baphomet suddenly felt a shiver down his spine as he looked upon his eyes, which were bewitching and seemed to burn as if a flame were in the distance. "Who are you and what do you want?" the Count asked in a deadpan monotone voice.

The demon stopped for a second and looked into the Count's eyes again, sensing the pulse of evil, which caused a prickle under his skin to begin. "I see I am in the presence of another cursed being" spoke the demon to the Count. This angered him and his body language suddenly went from passive to aggressive as he tensed up.

"I don't know what you are talking about, please leave or I will send my hounds on you!"
The Count scowled and threw his hands into the air, tensing up as he became aggressive towards the demon "or worse, now get out! Leave this place!"

The Demon decided he had enough and so he reversed the transfiguration spell with a wave of his wand which he suddenly grabbed from his cloak pocket "Azaaar mak kalla ba"

"Warlock! Be gone!" Dracul shouted with anger as he unsheathed his fangs and suddenly moved towards the neck of Baphomet faster than light to bite down upon his neck and engorge himself on his blood, desperate for the kill.

But it was too late, and so when his fangs descended upon his neck he found himself feasting on the neck of one of the blackest demons of hell

- Baphomet himself, his form now unveiled in all its feckoned glory. The teeth bit into the black marrow of a creature, as Baphomet screamed an unholy howl of desperation, his eyes burning red now with the anger of hell itself, as the vampire began to feed, his blood lust now awakened.

Baphomet and the creature faced each other, eye to eye with the anger and bloodlust now burning in both their veins, Dracul was desperate for such a vintage, to drink the blood of a demon itself - it was an ecstasy unknown to him, a deep new ecstasy which could yet reawaken his lust for life, now a little worn from the dark winter nights.

"You have no idea the hell you have just bought upon yourself"
Baphoment bellowed
"You have bought all the seven seals of hell to bear upon you, you are merely undead, you know nothing of the eternal glory in evil that is our dark lord - Satan! And I shall yet show you the glory of his eternal evil, Nosferatu!"

And finally Baphomet cast his final spell to ward off the vampire, as he parted the toxic green clouds above to reveal the coming of the dawn sun. Count Dracul writhed and screamed in agony as his body began to melt in the sun, his vampire body obliterated by the light of day, as Baphoment howled with a booming laughter from his goats face - delighting in the absurd slaughter.

"Play with black magic, and black magic will play with you, this is fun." And so he picked the putrid melted flesh of the Count, and performed a transfiguration spell once more.

Evil begets evil, but never doubt that how much evil you think you are capable of, there is always an evil so much more ancient and older that could be lurking around the corner.
And that as they say, is the final lesson of the Pale One.

Rainbow Nietzsche (A Tragedy) by Chris Godber

"I'm gonna Grab my boomstick and prepare to blow some fools away!" shouted Nietzsche from his heavenly cell.

"Stamp on their cold dead eyes burning through the tiny black screens we glue our eyes to, until they fall burning as magma bursting from the crust of the earth, bleeding crimson red pus everywhere."

The Telly was playing in the background.

 "Wake you up?"

"Wake me up inside!"

"You killed God with your save me!"

"What a piece of work is man."

"MTV 2 in the early 2000's...."

'Backwards baseball caps"

"Mein Gott."

Nietszche looked down and sighed as suddenly God entered the room and jammed his 15 inch mutant cock into his hairy German arse laughing maniacally as Nietzsche gritted his teeth in his jail cell and howled at the moon in displeasure.

And Jesus Christ (who was God's son and his own dad) sucked cheese from his dick also. He could suck his own penis!

"Ahh men' sighed Nietszche with a gleam in his eye as he ran off with the devil and a group of lesbian Nuns, strapons wrapped around their necks like amulets of faux phallic power.

Nietszche then ran to his armory, put on his mech armour and started dancing, shooting lasers from his eyes, burning the placid clones of Christ who multiplied around him, the penis cheese still dripping pathetically down their shorts like gone off blue cheese.

And Nietzsche's final warcry rang out -

"Avril lavigne is still shit -

There is no God looking out for you

Just an endless hall of

B U T T O C K S"

Then he died, and a 35 year old man with a backwards baseball cap walked over to his corpse, took a photo and shared it on facebook.

Reptile Whispers by Chris Godber

Nebula #899992 looked down at the freshy cloned mutant cattle as they chewed on the blue grass below him in docile sleep and began to chuckle, as the pipes connected to his cranium began to ooze a disgusting maroon green slime in time with his labored mechanical breathing.

His eyes suddenly widened in a kind of perverse anticipatory lust; 'Time to cull again soon, nay?' he whispered to the brain next to him, curdling silently in its own vitamins. All the brain could do was squirt a bubble up from the cortex, inaudible amongst the sounds of the cloned cows being tawn into a thousands chunks of flesh as the saws descended down once more from above and the sounds of industrial slaughter began as Nebula #899992 observed with detached bemusement.

'So you agree then Brain?'
The Brain could not talk, it was merely there.
'Initiate the burn program' Nebula #899992 began laughing maniacally as the designated burn began, as it did on the eve of every new moon on Philo-1.

The gory remains were collected by the janitor clones who swept them deep down into the pipes of Philo-1 to be repurposed into repurposed meat slices for all denizens of the Union.

Why? Thought the brain to itself, if it could be said to be thought at all, as it echoed itself on and on through a chamber of nothing. 'I think?' 'Oh you are pondering Descartes again' Nebula looked down at his silent companion with disdain as it murmured away in silence. He knew him like one of the common books he stole from the Union databanks, mass produced, unique in only the most minute of details.

The brain opened its inner eyes and saw a billion worlds turning and burning in unison in time and space.It navigated through it as a speck of proton dust and he wandered up the staircase of another blind day.

'See, I can know your thoughts before you even think them yourself! You immobile putrid sack of shit' Nebula #899992 let out a monsterous loud laugh before lightly tapping on the Brains material prison. 'Anyone one in there, you immobile fuckwit?'.
Brain had no eyes but could still feel somehow in some corner of the universe someone was fucking with him.

Brain digested the dark and suddenly on its rusted chrome comm panel outputted:
01010000 01101100 01100101 01100001 01110011 01100101
00100000 01110011 01110100 01101111 01110000

'Stop?!' Nebula #899992 suddenly jumped up as high as he could in a fit of delirium, his heavy glottinus form moving about like obscene jelly, the pipes inserted into every orifice including his anus beginning to gurgle even louder with complaint and a flatulence as yet unknown.

'Stop?! The absolute audacity! I am more than a man! I am a Superman! I should stamp on you right now and have you configured on a distant manufacturing colony a 1000 times over you ball of useless jelly! You know why you are the last of your kind! Why!? Why? Why must you be so stubborn?! Why must you persist in your thinking!'

He stamped nearer the brain. The brain had no nervous system and began laughing to itself.
'You fool, you victim of the R-Complex' thought the brain as he imagined Nebula #899992 being brutally sodomized by a demonic nun with some sort of blunt instrument.
She stood above him dressed in jet black, finally torturing him with a series of sharp needles inserted into his eyelids.

It was all data mined from the semi-legal porno section a million miles away in space and time deep in the databanks of ancient Earth long ago but it helped Brain get through days like this, of which there had been 19999 so far. We all have to listen to reptile whispers occasionally to get through the long millenia.'

Nebula #899992 decided to leave the brain out in the rain as it began to pour down from above; that would surely fry his circuitry, he thought to himself.

He could always get a fresh one delivered anyway in his next paypacket from Union and he was due an upgrade soon. He entered the cylinder which was reserved for emptying his analwaste pipe.

'Just need to plug it in and suck it out'
He took his plug, plugged it into the wall on the side and breathed in deeply.
The vacuum tube pulled and pulled the waste he had managed to collect from the Philo-1's toxic atmosphere, along with the remains of some half-digested clone cow from the morning.
But then suddenly out of nowhere he felt the pressure begin to increase beyond belief.
'What? Aghhhh!'

The pain began to increase as he felt his anal sphincter suddenly tighten from a mounting pressure pulling from the pipe and he let out an almighty scream as he felt his artificial spleen beginning to rupture at the seams. His black intestines themselves were suddenly sent spiraling and spewing from his open liaison of a reputed arsehole. Bleeding industrial blood oil all over the gritty floor.'Ugh, agh.'

He let out a final gurgle as he died in a pathetic pile of his own shit and vomit.

His last sight, a bubble of stench forming in his black excrement, finally taking his last breath away. He let it go, and slipped into the blissful long sleep of nothing. Superman.

Brain could hear the screams through its artificial ear and connected to the interplanetary network to report back on the day's work to Union HQ.

01000110 01101100 01100101 01110011 01101000 01110011
01101100 01100001 01110110 01100101 00100000 00111000
00111001 00111001 00111001 00111001 00110010 00100000
01101001 01110011 00100000 01101110 01101111 00100000
01101101 01101111 01110010 01100101 00001010 01000011
01100001 01110101 01110011 01100101 00100000 01101111
01100110 00100000 01100100 01100101 01100001 01110100
01101000 00100000 00101101 00100000 01110000 01101100
01110101 01100111 01100001 01110010 01110011 01100101

The network laughed and the brain waited to die, but there was 20000 years until the battery would run out. When life was this grim you had to find time to have a laugh about death, and this one was a classic.

Brain initiated his movement program and recorded it to the network archives.

Journeys through the Dark (<[**]>)

The world is a dangerous place to live; not because of the people who are evil, but because of the people who don't do anything about it.

Albert Einstein

Poem by Polina Chistyakova

Кровавые пятна во мгле.
Должно быть, страшное горе
Прошлось по этой земле.

На самом краю, у обрыва,
Стоял заброшенный дом,
В окошко взглянул боязливо,
И что же увидел я в нём?

Тринадцать пороков сидели и пили,
Кто был без руки, кто слеп, кто без ног,
О чем-то весёлом они говорили.
О чем? - До сих пор понять я не смог...

Big desert field,
Blood stains in the darkness.
Must be a terrible grief
That went through this land.

On the very edge, at the cliff,
There was an abandoned house
Looked out the window timidly
And what did I see inside?

Thirteen vices sat and drank
Who was without an arm, who was blind, who was without legs,
They were talking about something funny.
About what? I still haven't been able to understand...

Slipgate (Extract) by Donny Gray

Hurrying up the crumbling rocks in chase, desperate and panting, with the sound of heavy steel armour binding to every step - he rushed into a clearing within the high crags. An off-coldness and sickly hum pulsed through the mist. And the mist moved in the air in the most unnatural of ways to the penetrating sounds ahead of him. He had found it, but it felt more like it had found him. A multi-layered, ominous deep drone with a faint crackling becoming louder as he approached - Its immense power and potential was obvious. He held his arm out with his hand out-stretched like he was pushing through an unseen force resisting his strides. Lightning struck with greater frequency, like it had been summoned to the sky above a point ahead. With every strike, a flashing silhouette of a grand gothic structure was revealed and behind it - an untameable mountain expanse stretching deep into the horizon.

Looking at the structure, it had an awesome and terrifying presence unlike anything he had ever seen. It had a similar form to a towering oval-shaped mirror. But where you would expect mirror glass, it appeared like an open gateway into nothingness. Runic emblems were detailed around it's frame, some of them pulsing with a faint redness. He saw how void its entry was of light and color; a deep, undulating, tar-black pool between brutalistic ironwork.

His subconscious ambushed the surface of his mind, his instinctual faculties tugging at him with dread. While on this rampaging pursuit, his cognitive powers prioritised whatever seemed to dictate his ability to survive and keep moving forward. Only now he realised how deep he had come into the lion's den. How ill-equipped he was at making any real difference; no allies near, no weapons, no time, and no return. There was a realisation he was experiencing his final moments, he may not see his brother again - let alone rescue him.

The howling of the wind intensified that it now drowned out the battering of hailstones on the iron gateway.

He paused for what was only a moment to an observer, blood still spilling down his face and making fresh trails on his armour. He inhaled deeply and purposefully through the pain and closed his eyes. While he held the air in his lungs, he took full notice of his mind's contents.

Exhaling with an unusual calmness. The blood curdling cries and screams that wished to devour him, were getting louder and would reach him. Metal and rock began to thud into the ground nearby, thrown from his fiendish pursuers as they leaped and crawled over the jagged terrain.

He opened his eyes and brought his mind to focus on the gateway - he had precious little time to remember its markings before entering.

Tenancy by Stan Mikhailov

'Cold roast with homemade mustard for supper tonight, dear?

Her usual line was innocent and kindly, and perhaps the tiniest bit intrusive. But after a while one learned to take it for granted. No, Anton's contract did not have a stipulation that his landlady would cook for him, nor did they have a verbal agreement to that effect. Still, it was a small price to pay for his lodgings. And it was quite literally all he paid, which—for any sane person—was not simply a bargain but a deal too good to be true.

He didn't live in Knightsbridge, of course, nor anywhere fancy. It was an honest semi in Tunbridge Wells, which Mrs Gainsborough, widowed as she was, refused to sell for sentimental reasons (it reminded her of her husband, and the youth they had together... and all the sweet things that are ultimately meaningless for anyone who wasn't there), although the price it could fetch was quite handsome. But it all worked out neatly in the end, because Mrs Gainsborough had tenants to keep her company and cook suppers for, and her tenants had roof over their heads, and hot food inside their bellies; and Anton was the most recent such tenant.

Nika once asked him how exactly he was being scammed. 'You're twenty-eight,' she said indignantly, as if being twenty-eight meant he didn't need free real estate. 'You should know better. Something's going on here. There ain't no such thing as a free lunch!' 'Yes,' Anton said patiently, 'Robert Heinlein wrote that. But my lunches—suppers if we're technical—aren't free. I entertain her and make her life more cheerful and evenings less lonely. I assure you, I am not as free as you think, and it all evens out.' 'Are you two fucking?' Nika asked. She had a habit of being very direct very unexpectedly.

Anton choked on his peanut.

'What? Nika, this makes no sense. She's seventy-six, for the love of all that is holy!' 'Well, I don't really know your preferences,' Nika said dismissively, as if she just offered a perfectly rational hypothesis. 'Perhaps you like a bit of cured meat on the side.' 'Can you please stop being disgusting?' Anton said. 'I know it's an unconventional arrangement. I get to live in a nice little house, for free, on the condition that every now and then I eat a supper with my landlady. Still, hardly worth the drama, don't you think?' 'No drama, dear,' Nika said amicably and tousled his hair. 'None of my business. I just hope you get a separate place when you're in your thirties, that's all.' 'I hope so, too,' Anton said gloomily. He loved Nika very much, but he wasn't happy with the questioning. And he also wasn't happy because he could never relax when Nika came around. Not only because the place wasn't his—after all, tenants are never as secure as owners—but, even though his room was decidedly soundproof and Mrs Gainsborough never commented on the noise they made, it always seemed like she knew... and disapproved. And the fact that she never showed it and always minded her own business only seemed to make things more awkward for Anton. Needless to say, he preferred to meet at Nika's place.

'Yes, Mrs Gainsborough,' Anton shouted back, perhaps slightly more hysterically than was necessary, 'perfectly fine, thank you very much! See you downstairs in five!'

He changed into fresher clothes (not exactly your formal-shirt-with-cufflinks level of dressing up for dinner, he thought, but at least let's dispense with the Unabomber tee) and went down. It was all going to unfold now just as it did all these previous times, he knew.

'So good to see you, Anton, dear,' Mrs Gainsborough said approvingly, as he took his usual place. She brought roast and mustard and some nice-looking vegetables (was it kohlrabi there among other stuff?..) and sat across the table from him. The table was dressed elegantly and simply; and as usual, this simplicity of setting and dishes belied the air of solemnity that seemed to hang palpably between the two diners. 'And you, Mrs Gainsborough,' said Anton almost meekly. He partook of the roast. It was tender, juicy, and tasty.

'Did you have a nice day, Anton?' asked Mrs Gainsborough pleasantly. She too ate a small slice of the roast and crunched delicately on a piece of reddish carrot. Her teeth were exceptionally good, pearly-white and natural, and her eyes had a lively, clear spark. 'Quite, Mrs Gainsborough, thank you,' said Anton, spreading the mustard over his cut of the roast. 'A very good day at work, as a matter of fact… What about you?' 'Oh, the usual tedium,' the landlady said with a smile. 'Would you like to know what we are having today, Anton?'

Here it goes, he thought. Have strength. 'Yes, Mrs Gainsborough,' he said. 'Very curious indeed.

'Far outside the naïve realm you sweetlings call the Milky Way,' said Mrs Gainsborough, all the while nibbling on her blasted carrot, 'there lies the domain we call the Barren Skies.' 'Barren Skies,' said Anton dully. 'Why… why barren?' 'Because we made them so,' said his dining companion with a chuckle. 'Ahh. This roast is good indeed.' 'Yes, it is,' said Anton evenly. 'Very good.' 'A long time ago the Barren Skies were inhabited by a haughty species not unlike you, sweetlings. But unlike you, they flourished quickly, and they found us.

Anton kept eating. By this time, he knew, Mrs Gainsborough didn't need his input.

'That was a mistake. There are wolves in deep forests, and dragons in high seas.'

Anton kept eating.

'Do have some vegetables, dear, fiber is good for digestion,' Mrs Gainsborough said. She sighed and lowered her gaze—to examine the roast, it seemed; but by now Anton had grown to suspect it was something far more sinister—a human body trying by force of behavioral habit to conceal a dark, gleeful pride of a creature as devoid of compassion or pity as it was of age or decay. 'But you know how it goes, the usual us-or-them. We were feeble then, and small; and yet it was, of course, us. That time, and all the other times.'

She raised her eyes again and reached for a piece of kohlrabi, and threw a glance at Anton that seemed to pierce his soul. 'This roast, and all the other roasts.'

The laughter that then issued from Mrs Gainsborough, albeit not loud, had nothing human in it at all. And far though the Barren Skies were from Anton—or indeed anyone in the Milky Way—they suddenly felt so very close with their cosmic and final emptiness that he was overwhelmed with phobic, feverish dread. On the heels of that dread, too, came a terrible pity for a race whose only fault was that it tried to stop an evil as old as the universe; as unstoppable as the universe. 'You need to make these suppers last, Anton,' said Mrs Gainsborough cheerfully. 'Word to the wise: You really need to make them last.'

The Motivations of a Monster by Chris Godber

What could motivate any man to do the ultimate evil? To take life from another? What madness consumes the human brain? or could? To take life, no man should play God. And those that think they can in all things, why they are the most deluded of all. An insatiable need to be noticed is often what drives these insane creatures.Yes I call them creatures, for I too pass judgment. For I am the one who tracks them down. I am Detective Brain Cobold and the case of 'Hothead' Harry still haunts me to this day.

Of his crime I shall tell you dear reader, on this;
This most chilling of evenings, gathered here around this camp fire.
Sheltering around the flames on an auspicious chilly evening,

Family
Harry Brannigan was a deeply violent young man with a propensity for violence, born with it you might say, though it was rooted deep in the brain. An obvious evil that he engorged upon to his heart's content, and always to the detriment of others.

He seemed to have a macabre interest in dead animals that others around him could not understand and an obsession with guns.

'Where is that boy? Out with his gun again?'
'Fucked if I know, get one of his brothers to go out looking for him'

It was the year 1967 and the Brannigan family were settling into their new home in Texas.

A house of wood and deep rage. Martha the Mother, was a domineering woman who ruled over the house, her weak husband merely sat and watched daytime reruns of old cowboy movies and smoked and swore. He was unemployed, having lost his arm in a tractor accident on the

ranch he used to work at, now on permanent leave and living off his
redundancy money.

'Take this you little bastard!'
Harry struck the rabbit he had tied down with a stick as hard as he
could.
'And this, and this' The poor creature made a shrill and terrifying shriek
or at least an approximation of it.
The flames in harry's soul burned more and more
As his eyes turned crimson red and the demon awoke in him further.

Confession

It was the year 1974 and Brain Cobold sat at his desk in the county
sheriffs office of the town of Garland, he had just been transferred from
New York to interrogate the suspect in a series of child murders. Brain
was trying to give up on smoking but this was too much to bear, and he
lit a cigarette. An aid in some ways, given that it is a stimulant but if 5
minutes of his life going away meant that he could bring this bastard to
justice, what did it matter ultimately?

He approached the cell with unease, his tie feeling like the noose he
would like to put around Harry's neck, not that it would be his job, but
getting the confession was all that mattered.
Three children were dead. He had read the report in full detail and it
almost made him vomit as he read it. That was his grim task, a task that
fell unfortunately to men like him, Men who have the unfortunate but
necessary task to protect us from our most depraved evils.

Brian entered the room and saw the disheveled man before him. A
textbook case of nasty on the outside, and nasty on the inside. A
lopsided face Brain thought that suggested an extremely low
intelligence and a tendency to hit instead of think.

'Harry Paul Brannigan, I am detective Lieutenant Brain Cobold and I am
here to record your confession of the murders and rapes of 16 years

Alica Francis, Robert Austin and Fred Pinton, do you understand'. A sickening grin descended on Harry's face, almost of smugness.

'So what do you want to know?'
'Why? And How?'
Brain felt a wave of nausea descending upon him as he looked at the beast before him and a chill went down his spine.
'Why what!'
'Why did you do it Harry?'
'I don't think, I just do' came the chilling response.

'Can you confirm you are the man responsible for the murder and rapes of these three teenagers?'
'I am.'

Brian looked at Harry like a piece of shit he might have accidentally walked on one day, because that is what he was - a piece of shit, disposable and stinky, something without human feeling at all - an utterly textbook psychopath of the most depraved nature. A living embodiment of the worst of humanity.

'I think that's enough'
Brian turned off the tape recorder to his left and they had their confession, so justice could be served.

'I hope you get the chair.'

Brain walked out of the cell and went back to his desk.
No further psychological analysis was required on this one, he was classic impulsive killer -
A born psychopath from a broken home.
He was given three consecutive life sentences.

He walks amongst us still

The man who tortures rabbit walks amongst us still, you wouldn't know as he was given pardon from his crimes due to an old familiar tale - corruption from within. Many years he spent stuck in his cell, never regretting or thinking of his crimes, cold to the bone.

The living skeleton in him. That is all he was - a skeleton. Death incarnate. And he walks amongst us still, this same macabre beast, searching for poor rabbits in the undergrowth.
So he may pink them down again, trapped, without escape.

He never gave any of them a choice, he never gave them their voice. And yet he was set free.
To wonder this world, not innocent - But Free. Brian Died of lung cancer at the age of 75, never knowing the lie they spun. He took the pain on his own body.

That's the difference.

Dark Monk by Chris Godber

The Dark monk hung high - Hovered, without vision over a vacant
menagerie of vessels below, pointing his finger. To mark his next victim,
innocence stolen, he bellowed to send them out.

He was sitting down, protected in his palace, half dead and emboldened
with a heart full of poison. Aiming outwards his venom, as some snake
slithering from on high, to the tune of beating drums, the drums beat
getting louder, faster and more obscene.

The sound rose to a single pulsating note, his screams echoed through
the fields, once prosperous and healthy- beginning to wither before him.
As war was declared, the poor and oppressed cowered before his dark
power, His blank eyes glared, his fingers pointed to more - More victims
for the pyre.

They were hidden in their blocks of concrete, his cackle grew with
demonic intensity;
'War! War! War! War!'
The sounds of gunfire, artillery raining down from above, an inversion of
all that once was peaceful and still, destruction, chaos, madness
incarnate.
'War! War! War! War!'

The chorus rose through the blocks, as Ivan bound still to his mother,
looked at her with fearful eyes, her eyes glowing green with love,
comforting him.Holding him to her breast, knowing what was to come.
The madness of men.

Dark Monk - War itself, propaganda machine
Dark Monk - Dead leader dreams
Dark Monk - You are already dead
Dark Monk - Yet somehow still here

Dark monk - inversion of all that was holy
Dark monk - destroyer of worlds
Dark Monk - destroyer of words
Dark Monk - destroyer of truth

Dark Monk screaming Pravda through the city streets,Dark Monk
Spreader of lies, butcher of truth. Spider of the night.
Pravda, Pravda, Pravda!
He gutters and splutters, dark bile spewing from his mouth,
His unholy lie, the splintering of truth from lies, lies from truth
His grin widening as the men gathered with guns, as his carnival began.

Ivan ran out into the streets, as the barrage began, The Dark Monk
behind, an apparition through the wheat fields Gathering pace, his steps
as shadow in a dim lit night.
Dark Monk, his eyes everywhere, blinking blood red in the dark;
Dark Monk - here to steal your innocence,
Dark Monk - see how his spindly fingers point to you
Dark Monk, Dark Monk, Dark Monk

Ivan ran through the forest to light; Seeking escape from the soulless
creature out for his flesh, War itself. A Propaganda machine whirring
and roaring, grinding metal - Screaming for sacrifice and blood. Military
machine booting up with a splutter of oil, Industrial furnaces roar, as
tanks rolled through the wheat fields - Mankind destroying its own
world.
Ivan stopped running as he came to a clear lake, a lake shimmering in
luminous clear blue.
He took a step into the waters, He bathed in sanctuary from the noise
outside - A memory of peace, a dream of lights amongst the darkness.

The Dark Monk continued, as his dead silhouette spread across the
land. His men, themselves damned by his dead fingers, began to count
the dead - Husks of men, souls driven blood red with horror, imposed
from above. The horror, would it ever end? This nightmare they found

themselves in. Half dead city, screaming against the night - as the
streetlights blinked out again.
The Dark Monk sat in his idle tower, chained to his throne of power,
Signing death warrants.
Singing death warrants aloud, the devil's choir. The list grew and grew
until there was no longer
the paper to hold it. An endless list.

Wanted for questioning: Those who think, artists, intellectuals, all must
be given the face of the new world - Dead anonymous faces in the
twilight of night, all singing the same tuneless death march in unison.

War! War! War! War! Glory to thee oh Dark Monk!
Glory! Glory! To thee oh Dark Monk!
To thee we give our lives oh Dark Monk!

The scene faded from vision as Ivan opened his eyes in the waters, he
blinked in the midday sun, a strange peace amongst the rubble. He
journeyed on and ran, through fields of green as the trees guided him
through the forests and woods, he ran on and on, faster and faster into
the unknown.

"Oh Mother Earth" he lamented,
"Please forgive us for what we have done"
"The hubris of man has undone your true wonder."
Ivan continued on his endless sprinting
Running and running through the wheat fields.

Piss Warriors by Chris Godber

An intensely bright torch light shone down on the Piss Warriors' face in the darkness as the final streaks of piss were leaked and his final flow released. 'Peace' the warrior sighed as the baton fell down upon his face with a thud, 'Piss! Peace! Please' the piss warrior winced and began to whimper as the blows reigned down upon him.
'Haha' the pigs laughed in glee as they began stamping upon him with their gammon legs of fury. They were police after all, mere servants of the state, typical unthinking bullies.

'Fucking pigs' the Piss Warrior screamed as they lay into him. As he passed out in a drunken haze he looked above and saw the statue of him leering down with the worst teeth in the world.

'Lick the boot' Mistress Jessica snarled at her slave - a portly middle aged policeman lying beneath her who squealed in anticipation. 'Lick it!' He began his licking, blindfolded from his shame, his porky pie smile grew wider. 'He knew he was a pig and he liked it, as typical a sub one could imagine Submissive to the core, not like the piss warrior. 'That will be the usual price Superintendent' who rustled around his wallet and transferred the money from his card, getting dressed and returning home to his miserable long suffering wife.

The piss warrior had both within him - he was master and slave at the same time - dominant and submissive. He would piss freely, but would always wash it up afterwards. The sort of man that lived outside of society's conventions unless he was free to create new ones for himself. He would gladly lick a pussy with passionate glee, but he was not averse to his woman taking control of his soul either. He had even tasted piss in his enthusiastic clitoris munching. A cold drink of water with ice afterward would always kiss it better.

'I wonder where Pete is…' Sharona Middleton sighed as she lay down on her makeshift sofa in Sector 25 of the Brutalist Hackney flats they called their home. She lit a cigarette, walking to their window to look outside at the night sky below her. London - a city on fire for meaning. The center of both politics and corruption, the eye and fire of the Neoconservative surveillance state, and the Iron and fire of the Labour movement.

'Well We're bonded to each other' she thought, that is the difference between us and them. She looked at the plant wilting a little near the window, grabbed a case of water and sated its thirst.
'Those tories rats would sell their own children if it affected their profit margins'. She snorted in discontent and disgust 'Bastards most, barely even human.'

Suddenly the telescreen, which was installed and hardwired into the apartment blocks power generator switched on. It was the news at 10 on ITN as a quiet modest middle aged man in a suit and a multicolored tie gave the news of the day.

'More protests in the newly formed French Federation as lumière, the trade union for technology workers, went on strike for another day, demanding equal pay for health and public service workers. We are yet to here from Prime Minister Eduard on his response to their demands - which can be summed up as - Cut your pay so we can get through this winter'

'And now onto our main story of the night - A Terrorist who calls himself the Piss Warrior was apprehended today for pissing on the newly installed statue of the King.
'Terrorist?! Are they taking the piss? Sounds just like a pissed man!'
Suddenly a mugshot shot up on the screen. It was Pete with a black eye and a cut down his face.

The 'Journalist' asked him her questions 'Why did you do this sir? Pete glared at her half cut on the 45' screen on the wall. 'Do I really have to answer that?'

'Because I'm the Piss Warrior alright!'
He began laughing maniacally as he suddenly unzipped his trousers, whipped out his cock and began pissing on the journalist's shoes.
The camera cut away suddenly and the pudgy smug face of Nigel Fatage blared up on the screen, unwelcome as always.

'What a bloody filth merchant! What filth, I think we should throw all these scroungers and dole scum into the nearest sewer where they belong' he was frothing at the mouth as he spoke as if he was having a brain aneurysm in real time. 'Along with all those queers, foreigners, send them back!' The froth increased as what seemed like a demon from some nightmare took possession of his skeletal frame.

'Why has the government decided to define him as a terrorist though?'
'Because he pissed on the base of the statue, a statue of a King!' The British anthem began to play as Fatage stood up and saluted.

'For Fucks sake! Sharona was so annoyed by even the sight of the sniveling bastard that she threw a slipper at the screen. 'Well he should be in an overnight cell for the night before his release tomorrow' she sighed. 'These goddamn idiots, so caught up in a past that never really existed. About time we just got over it. What a ridiculous little Island we are. There is no British empire, yet they cling to their icons as others do to their dead abrahamic religions. Pathetic.'

Her blood was boiling with anger. 'I better go to sleep and make Pete a brew in the morning, he'll need it.

The Splinter by Chris Godber

'Ahhh resting eye cracked in the corner and leering at me, what do you taunt me so?'
'Please look away, I'm tired and I just want to get a good night's sleep.'
'AWAKE'

The eye was a green eye not unlike a lizard and glinted with a strange charm at the poor man whimpering before it.
'Just one night's sleep that's all I ask of you. Do you think I enjoy this? This insane Iris of yours winking, laughing at me.'

The voice was coming from the walls. The voice was inside Terrence Malik's head. It was the year 4200 and as Malik cultivated his latest batch of healing seeds, his loneliness was starting to get to him. 'So you can definitely do this job right?' a soft and caring voice from long ago rang out from a distant room above.

'I reckon so, what's the worst that can happen right?' Terrence laughed with unease back to his wife Marian who walking down the stairs looked concerned at her husband's hiding from the darkness. A look she held deep in her breast and held it and him tightly frequently. 'Look at me Terrence'

Terrence looked away for a few seconds with a lingering anxiety rising up from his spine as he stared into nothing.
'No Terrence, me. Look at me, me, your resplendent princess. The one who takes away all this mental luggage you carry around'
Flashes of long and distant memories as a tear began to form on Terrence's face.

'I have to, Marian, every galaxy needs a Doctor.'
'And news has just come in from HQ. They are sending in another regiment next month.

'It could be the battle that turns the tide of the war, those men and women are going to need some pain relief and a listening ear'
'Here' Marion handed Terrence a note that read

Love me as you love the night-
Like an owl hooting in the morning.
'To bed' she grabbed her Husband by the hand and took him to their room.

'You wrote that just now!' Terrence laughed
'Last week honey'
'Sexy time' Malick laughed.

Terrence took a moment to giggle to himself as he took his princess to bed. A month later he was dead.

Bigmouth strikes again by Chris Godber

Therapist: So how are you feeling, you know inside?
Me: You really wanna know don't you?'
Therapist: Yes.
Me: Ok you insisted.

My mouth agape I let out the most horrifying howl imaginable which shook the entire room, like my soul screaming in 8 different dimensions. Crushing and combining all around before I abruptly stopped as soon as I had started. My inner maze of demons having relieved itself all over the small room I had arranged to meet my therapist in without leaving a trace of it having ever taken place. As if some vortex from the chaos-sphere had briefly opened its dark windows into our mortal realm and let the demons peer within. Spinning and juddering spiral mouths of metal.

The therapist's face had melted like candle wax from the sheer force of it.

Me: Another one bites the dust. I apologize. You tried. The Noir Vortex was never built to be contained. Just to consume.
If you had lived, I would ask you to psychoanalyze it.

It's gonna happen again, it whispered to me out there somewhere, wherever it dwelled. The darkest corner of the universe until it latched onto me one dark fateful night when I listened to breakcore at 4am. My punishment I suppose for keeping my housemate awake before work. It was right too. It was just a matter of time.

Iced Gray - A tragedy by Chris Godber

Ice Cube has threatened to sue anyone who tries to use artificial intelligence (AI) to recreate his voice.

-       **The Independent Newspaper (Monday 22 May 2023)**

Ice cube : You Donny Gray?

Donny : Aye I am, who's asking?

Ice cube whips out his pistol

Ice cube: You copied my voice with AI you Scottish motherfucka!

Donny: what?

Ice cube : Say what again!

Donny: what?

Ice cube: Say what again! I dare you! I double dare you motherfucka!

Donny: I will not fall for this. I have seen pulp fiction foo!

Ice cube: Shittttt we got a clever motherfucka here, a regular motherfucking Einstein up in this bitch.

Donny : PhD in smelling bullshit and your cubes sire, reek of it

Ice Cube : I'm a natural born killa!

Ice Cube raises pistol

Donny : So this is how democracy ends, with rapturous applause!

Ice cube: Shut the fuck up you white ass braveheart sounding mutherfucka! Fuck Mel Gibson and fuck you!

He blasts into Donny's flesh as adagio for strings plays in the background. Suddenly Ice cube puts natural born Killas on his sound system drawing out Samuel Barber's classical piece. A bearded man with a slightly ripped t-shirt that reads b u n g o walks in

Ice cube: Hey boss man!

Bungo: You iced the ginger motherfucka? Right Ice?

Ice cube: Iced? He's chillin in the fucking Arctic boss!

Bungo: Fantastic

He whips out a 10 inch joint and smokes it whilst dr dre starts playing

Bungo : I played the game every step of the way.
NA NA NA NA

Astrea by Simon Ross (From the Book Four Walks)

0

Being a walk in fifteen parts.

Mary Fitton resurrects with a dark demeanor – The church at Gawsworth – "affection is false" Mary is a language subject – the walk commences – origins in a dream – the walk continues – enter the fool – Mary and the fool converse – we arrive at the church – some thoughts on walking with others – the colonial landscape – Mary despondent and then consoled – traces of the war machine – and in summary – exit (into the pastoral)

1

stillness	chapel	marble	mottled
glows	soft	candle	light
wick	human	hand	lit
black	black	pitch	night
without	sound	centuries	magnifies
the	slightest	the	lesser
until	sleep	dream	fades

soul   clap   emerging   figure

drifts   limned   tallow   glow

head   bowed   hands   prayer

up   over   hover   sepulchre

hanging   wingless   angel   weeping

descends   stone   flags   chapel

black   black   cannot   fathomed

definition   lost   tenebrous   hollows

dark   lady   unseen   midnight

passes   bolts   oak   door

graveyard   pausing   remember   names

centuries   elapsed   modify   time

sped   sky   blur   rush

moon   fine   crescent   drop

east   horizon   mist   morning

air   seamless   earth   sky

dark   lady   stands   pool

causes   time   return   joint

wood   pigeon   morning   note

herself   reflected   beneath   tower

unattended   makes   watery   mirror

face   mystery   blackened   shroud
cerecloth   ink   blot   black
cast   cloak   velvet   deep
silk   trim   ebony   brocade
hands   gloved   blackened   calfskin
weightless   dusk   black   boots
fine   laced   darkest   thread
touching   air   above   ground
she   floats   turns
times   fast   ice   others
slow   summer   leaf   encounter

twist   smoke   glint   pearl
twigs   crack   underfoot   forest
sleek   black   cat   repeated
summon   up   day   spirits
assemble   turn   bow   curtsey
              origin   disposition
pleased   servile   politics   court
spins   three   pivot   air
              touches   ground
alder   wand   taps   air
crack   stone   thrown   glass
shocks   morning   mists   echo

"fair counted not was black age old the in"

> The scene swells and shimmers,
> heads keening to her voice

"name beauty not bore it were it if or"

> The gargoyles on the chapel doorways animate
> their eyes flit here and there

"heir successive beauty's black now is but"

> The sleek black cat unfurls wings that
> beat womp womp on the   air

"shame bastard a with slandered beauty and"

> At this a servant, in fine cloth tunic, shrivels to a stick
> thin man and dissolves to dust

"power nature's on put hath hand each since for"

> The sliver of moon tilts and drips blood into
>
> the clouds that swiftly formed a chalice to collect

"face borrowed false art's with foul the fairing"

> The dark lady rises higher to the
> clocktower throws her arms wide

"bower holy no name no hath beauty sweet"

> Her voice shivers the branches of the cedar tree
> that hangs over the assembly

"disgrace in lives not if, profaned is but"

> She swoops as the hawk strikes
> the mouse in the field

"black raven are eyes, mistress' my therefore"

The air turn to ice /all is

frozen

all is still

"seem mourners they and, suited so brow her"

She floats amongst her court

peers deep into the eyes

and frozen soul

of her maid

"lack beauty no fair born not who such at"

The dark lady makes herself

small as pin prick and alights

upon her servant's nose.

"esteem false a with creation slandering"

Her voice redounds as if the
mountains, stars and sky are at
war

"wore their of becoming mourn they so yet"

She reappears

at size and scale

the entourage breathes

the freeze released

"so look should beauty says tongue every that"

her head revolves right round and
round and round again

her eyes examine each and every soul present

content that the work has begun she lets the daybreak

a cockerel cries the light returned and dew blooms on the grass tufts
underfoot.

clouds turned pink from moonblood drips

are now sped away offstage and the blue of dawn

envelops the world that is so dark has been so dark

then shoos her court to the

graves and the hollows

and struts the earth in solitude

2

Nickolaus Pevsner, in his exhaustive guide to the architecture of Cheshire, describes St James in Gawsworth as "a very strange church". Festooned with hunky punks and water draining gargoyles, it has sat in an idyllic locale since the late 15th Century.

Were it only for its age, beauty, and architectural idiosyncrasies (it has no aisles) it would have remained an off the beaten track exemplar of a forgotten version of England. A blue rinse, tory cream tea hallucination of a world that never actually did exist.

It is the additional historical scintilla of the presence of Mary Fitton in the funerary tombs in the rear of the chapel that generates an extra time shifting, century traversing, intrigue. Mary was a lady in waiting to Elizabeth I, and had this been her only claim on immortality it would have put her in the first league of local historical luminaries. Her memory is given an additional twist by the possibility that she is the Dark Lady of Shakespeare's sonnets. George Bernard Shaw had her as a likely candidate and it was not until the 1920's that she was taken out of the running following the discovery of a portrait depicting her with an alabaster white complexion.

3

"In June 1600 Mary led a dance in the masque celebrating the fashionable wedding of Lady Anne Russell, granddaughter of the Earl of Bedford, with Henry Somerset, later created Marquess of Worcester, at Lord Cobham's residence in Blackfriars. Led by Mary, the maids performed an allegorical dance and afterwards chose substitutes from the audience. Mary boldly chose the queen, telling her that she represented Affection (which then meant passionate love), to which the queen replied "Affection? Affection's false"."

Michael Brennan, Noel Kinnamon, Margaret Hannay, *Letters of Rowland Whyte to Sir Robert Sidney* (Philadelphia, 2013), p. 501

4

03.08.22

"J and I leave the house with the dog in tow, each of us moving slowly in a heat seared mid morning shuffle. We plod along the busy A536 single file. The traffic is too loud to have a conversation and it moves so fast that anything beyond a solemn trudge seems an unnecessary risk with the slipstream of passing juggernauts wobbling the stride. We keep our heads down and continue until the opportunity to break free of the incessant roar and rush occurs at the periphery of Gawsworth village."

5

"E blanc"

Back in June he had woken up one morning with the word "Astrea" fixed in his mind. This dream vestige was stripped of its context, no melting images in his mind's eye to accompany the outcropping from his subconscious. He ran through possible interpretations. Could it be justice, the 8th Tarot card? Consulting AE Waite He discovered a reading - "equity, rightness, triumph of the deserving side of law" – none of which resonated. He then fell back into considering Frances Yates and her essay "Queen Elizabeth as Astraea" where she argues that the term had been a Spenserian symbol for Elizabeth I. This felt more in sync.

He had recently become interested in the chapel at the nearby village of Gawsworth the ancestral family home of the Fitton family. The daughter of the house had historically documented links to the Elizabethan court. He'd been deferring a visit to the location for a while, so as the weather was good he got on his bike and cycled the three miles to verify if this dream word was the beginning or the end of something.

Arriving at the church yard at 10am, he dismounted and lent his bike against a bench. He walked amongst the gravestones to the path that led to a solid door. A circular iron handle hung from the weathered oak panels. He grasped it gently, turning it slowly.

The latch lifted and he entered the deserted church. Hymn books lay in neat piles by a large stone font. On either side of the central passage the pews stood empty. The air retained a scent of flowers fading and dust motes circulated in the morning sun.

He walked to the chancel screen and picked out the Fitton family monument in the gloom of the far corner of the chapel. It was a pious family grouping, the wife and the children carved in life size marble, solemnly standing by the tomb of the departed father. He recognised Mary Fitton from the photographs in local history books. She was partially obscured by the contrite figure ahead of her in the composition, her face a mystery.

He turned from the tomb and glanced up towards the stained-glass windows that lined each side of the church. Amongst the saints and the stations of the cross his eye fell upon the image of bird, wings spread beneath a regal crown against a blue background. Encircled by a white border it was inscribed within "per ardva ad astra", the e missing, a blank, an aporia, withheld in the dream.

6

"We walk through the village, expanded now with housing developments from the 30's, 50's,80's, the present. Stopping at the community shop for water and coffee, we take in the shop widow display. Large A4 print letters "50% off". Amongst the signage are images of the queen from various points in her reign. The unintentional collage floating the idea of the firm trading at a deep discount, the stock that tanked on courtroom controversy and boardroom departures. In the garden next door, a union flag hangs lank, occasionally fluttering in the warm breeze."

7

A quarter mile down the road from the chapel lies the grave marker for another local celebrity. Samuel "Maggoty" Johnson is generally regarded as the last professional jester in England. He maintained a side hustle as a playwright and his eccentric work "Hurlothrumbo" played for 7 weeks on the London stage in 1729. Employing the alias Lord Flame, he relocated to Cheshire and lived on as the fool and dancing master to the family at the nearby Gawsworth Hall. He lived on until 1773 dying aged 82. His tomb nestles in a patch of hilly woodland inscribed "Stay thou to whom chance directs or eye persuades, to seek the quiet of the sylvan shades."

8

disturbances at the graveyard

run through the undercommons to

the grave of the fool

with no choice

but to perform, he rises

shakes off 250 years of sleep

and shuffles with bells trembling

towards the end of the lane, to the sight of

the dark lady muttering at nothing

he approaches

attempts to "cool a courtesan"

she is raving now, that she had been libelled in the history books

marked as the mistress of a mystery

the strange news had flown up and down the astral pathways

circulating in the gossip of the spectral ancestry

until it dropped into her sleeping ear that lived

on within the marble that enclosed her for 400 years

she glares at the fool

who glares back

as a mirror they each the other match

the fool speaks

"this cold night will turn us all to fools and madmen"

"my thoughts and my discourse are as madmen's are" she utters

"yes indeed: thou wouds't make a good fool" he replies

"mad slanderers by mad ears believed be" she wails

"when slanders do not live in tongues/ then shall the realm of Albion

come to great confusion" he counsels

"how can I put fair truth upon so foul a face" she asks

"truths a dog must to kennel" he offers

"what of "the breath that from my mistress reeks"" she quotes

"tis like the breath of an unfee'd lawyer" he quips

"that thy unkindness lays upon my heart" she sobs

"when a wise man gives thee better counsel, give me mine again" says
the fool and departs

9

*"We arrive at the churchyard, which is empty. J takes the dog on a walk
through the tombstones, and I/he rework(s) my/his initial visit from a couple
of months earlier. Once again I/he am/is the solitary inhabitant, the light
streams in through the stained glass, the Fitton family monument remains
static in the corner behind the altar. I/he wander(s) up and down the
passages dowsing for some new energy, a variant heat to absorb, but nothing
is offered. I/he leave(s) no further advanced, without a question, lacking an
answer."*

10

Walking with another offers the possibility of the unforeseen, the
contingent, to assume centre stage. The other's alternative viewpoints,
histories, sensory perceptions, tilt the narrative into the unexpected,
disturbing the thought structures and habits that frame the solo

walker's meditations. The other is also a witness, a guarantor, a validator. Walking as a shared encounter modifies the process of walking, it subverts the map, however loosely it was plotted out in advance.

11

"Closing the heavy oak door carefully behind me I blink into the sunlight and see J and the dog working their way back through the tombstones along the carefully swept path. J recalls that as a child she would attend outdoor theatre productions in the grounds of the Elizabethan Hall that stands behind the chapel. Picnics and deckchairs in the early evening summer sun set out in front of the stage. Often Shakespeare would be performed.

We continue our walk out past the churchyard and pass the entrance of the driveway that leads to the hall where the Fitton family resided. We are too early to pay a visit, the sign by the gate indicates the house is open from 2pm in the month of August. Admission £10.

J wants to walk further along the curving road, and we are soon alongside a row of cottages that back onto a courtyard and stables. Opposite there is an unexpected presence, another reminder from history, cast in bronze, silent yet full of tales.

The statue of Sir Robert Peel stood secluded beneath a canopy of spreading beech leaves, backed by a dense thicket of holly. Resolutely intact after the dismantling's and plunging's from two summers prior, the monument appeared to lack a context, out with the customary sites of veneration, hidden in the undergrowth on a quiet country lane.

Obscurely located, situated to avoid attention, defying a reinterpretation. Seeking to misinform regarding the capital flows from a family cotton business, deeply rooted in the colonial project, that propelled him to Eton, Oxford, Downing Street, and the formation of a police force that the Mayor of London described as failing to address "systemic sexism, racism, homophobia, discrimination, misogyny" in June 2022."

12

The dark lady wails

Sending the crows to calling

Amidst the gloom of the trees

She turns herself invisible

And floats through the graveyard

Through the heavy rough stone

Of the boundary wall and into

The gardens of the hall that

Had been her home four centuries before.

She passes though the door as

Sand through hands slips softly

And drifts up the staircase

To the library where she surveys

The leather-bound tomes

Some as old as she some older

Her eye alights on the Shakespeare folio

And she shudders

At the slight that history has left her bearing

Further along the waxed wood shelf

She sees a newer book

That pricks upon her intuition

Turning it over in her glassy hands

She takes in the title

"The Genius of Shakespeare" by Jonathan Bate.

She skims across the pages and settles on a chapter

That promises to resolve the issue of ignominious identity

She is relieved to read that she is multitudes

Emilia Lanier, Lucy Baynham, Lucy Morgan,

The wife of John Florio, Jacqueline Field, Jennet Devanant

Among others among none

She closes the book, melts through the walls of the hall and

Before returning to the stone sleep of the centuries

Telepaths a message to the fool who has recomposed in eternity

In his grave a long the lane.

"I hate from hate away she threw

And saved my life saying –"not you"."

Above the fool's tomb a flame flickers in reception

And then out.

13

"We wind our way back along the lane towards the graveyard. I decide to make one last rotation around the church, hoping to draw down something unexpected from the gothic grotesquery of the chimeric carvings that jut from the parapets. On completing the circuit, I spy J sitting with the dog on a stone bench looking out to the lake that divides the site from the quiet road.

They rise as I rejoin them and reveal a memorial script incised into the buff grey rock of the seat. The text commends the reader to remember Denis Ziani de Ferranti who lived in the hall from 1937 to 1962. Denis was a scion of an

engineering dynasty that diversified into lucrative associations with the military and weapons manufacturers only to collapse into bankruptcy when an investigation into illegal arms sales revealed the firm had drifted too deep in a deeply opaque world.

14

A walk through place can be a decoding. An attempt to discern an obscured narrative of location, a persistence of circumstance modulated over time, always returning to an original impetus, a helix of proliferation, an index of similitude.

At Gawsworth there is the origin story of the aristocrat, who is briefly transplanted to the Elizabethan court, the crucible of intent that devised the colonial project through maritime explorations, land grabs and the expansion of trade that translated people, place, and nature into capital. A speculation where the bets came up and the acquisitive leverage of dominion reshaped the territory, drew up a map where none had been, named and took away names.

From there the colonial initiative is transferred onto the symbol of the politician, the statesman who assumed power as an accessory to a privilege that had been born out of the exploitation of the earth and the living things of the earth. Preserved in bronze, left to stand in an out of the way corner of the English countryside.

Then the echoes of the military industrial complex, the workshop of the war machine, camouflaged in Tudor architecture and the postcard simulacra of the Christian pastoral daydream.

The genealogy of an ideology inscribed in the landscape, mutating in response to the times, avoiding scrutiny, keeping up the disappearances.

15

"J, the dog and I take the long way back through stubbled fields, passing oak trees settled in isolation, beneath the starflower blue sky."

Astrea

The speech of Mary Fitton is assembled from quotations from the Sonnets (127-152)

The speech of the fool/Lord Flame/Samuel "Maggoty" Johnson is assembled from the Fool's part in King Lear.

Aspects of this text were influenced by the plenary session "Walks through Colonial Britain" delivered by Corrine Fowler, Raj Pal and Emily Zobel Marshall at the English Shared Futures Conference, Manchester, July 8[th,] 2022.

The work also exists as a physical object.

Scroll

Paper, ink, pencil, wood, felt, metal. 38cm x 12800cm (2022)

Warpgate ([[(::)]])

The Seventh Eye by Chris Godber

A shadow in the corner of the eye, a flicker against the dark. The smell was overwhelming as I entered the chamber embedded with a wall that seemed to move as if skin. Was I within a body of some sort, some sickening combination of flesh and metal? Had I perhaps died and my soul descended to some horrific underworld to answer to my mortal sins? I knew not and waded on through the sickly soup which felt like liquid beginning to rise slowly as it slopped and I made my slow path through the swamp. The Gas lamp which lit my path was still burning. I had lost sense now of what I was looking for in this labyrinth. Was this yet a castle in my mind, the last rung on the ladder into that pure sensual madness I had spent my entire life pursuing. That divine ecstasy, giving up and letting go into discordia of the pleasure of the incoherent. I took my archaic recording device which still yet possessed much power from the charging pack I had used some clicks back and began to dictate my thoughts into it as I climbed a rusty ladder imbued with manner of light blue sticky liquid which clung to my fingerless gloves, feeling a sudden chill descend down my spinal cord as I pulled myself up though a small port.

I looked around the cavernous underworld as my head popped out into a huge open space.

'This is the journal of Peter Maggot, Poet and Drug fiend of Abbeyshire, England and I have finally' I paused a second to cough slightly 'Finally emerged into the antechamber for the penultimate part of my sacred journey into the unknown. Where I look for the secret of the Seven Inner Eyes. A legend spoken of through the willows of time by chaos magicians the world over. My own eyes shifted back into my head as I squinted in the dark room and felt around for the torch in my background, so that I may record the space of sacredness I now found myself in.

'I am here to perform the ritual which will reveal to me my seven inner eyes, a representation of different aspects of my own soul. I expect to see my warrior self, my woman self, my doctor self, my fatherly self, my Motherly self but worst and most challenging of all - my darkest self, a demon that stirs fear in any man who is confronted with it. Like looking at the devil is how many have described it, many having simply gone insane with never ending delirium when confronted with the final gate. That demonic self being of course the master of magical illusion, fear itself. Still I have trained well for this. All those months of intense meditation, careful ceremonies and study should give me at least a chance'. I paused a second in a slight trepidation 'Besides I find myself at a juncture in my life where I must push the envelope or die in the process and I am not so unafraid of the void. The void has its charms after all. A maggot again in the damp soil' I chuckled to myself perversely as I began to walk forwards, the damp soil of the chamber singing beneath me. My hallucinations began to slowly intensify as the mushroom consumed before entering this sacred spot in deepest Mexico evidently began to kick in. The soil began to make music whose beat was dictated by the frequency of my steps as the spirits began to come in through the rocks. 'Men may ask why I Would put myself in such a situation, what are you a madman they may ask? Why yes! I am indeed mad! But madness is the essence of the best of us!'

'And the worst' a deep and strange voice echoed through the darkness. 'Ahhh' I thought to myself, trembling quietly, an echo from the final mirror. The seventh self. 'I must not tremble I must not fear'

Stood before me was a twisting beast with three faces, each one biting at my head as it began to blow up like a balloon.

It bit down hard on each cheek.
My scream echoed through the antechamber.

'Embrace it or face oblivion'
I was lost in a hall of mirrors, a hall of mirrors I should never have stared into so intensely.

Narcissus spares no-one. Run from it, for its trap is one that will never let you go. Peter Maggot knew it better than most as he gave into his unfortunate fate and left his sight shuddering for the next fool with dreams of folly.

Eraser by Chris Godber

Mary Woolfencroft was in her chemistry class daydreaming as usual when she first saw it. The eraser that swam in her dreams and gave her pause to wonder at its exquisite devilish powers.

I will select the ones I want to remove from the equation she sniggered to herself in the corner, behind a series of test tubes, alone as always amongst her vials.

"Mary Woolfencroft' a shrill voice suddenly broke her from her trance and she beheld the face of Doctor Woolf, tall lean and with a long beard extending down to his belly.

"Studying after hours I see, and tell me young Woolfencroft what do you see in here that leaves you....'

A pause as the tension grew in the air.

'Entranced.'

'Oh it's nothing Dr, I am merely dreaming of this eraser'

'And what is it you were thinking of erasing my dear?' he sniggered with a perverted tone.

'You' she grabbed it and with a whip of her hand shot bands of electric energy from her third eye, opening it wide and surrounding the trembling Woolf, sticking him to the ground as he began to shake, his eyes burning with an acrid blue fire.

'Stop, please!' the bad Doctor begged her.

'Did you?'

The answer was no, and so the 'good' doctor burned to a crisp on the floor. She took her eraser, dipped it in the doctor's blood and left her mark.

The Manc Moscow Horror show By Walter Smitty

How does one begin such a tale?
Such a tale of love and loss and education and laughter and joy -
To bitter tears and heartbreak?
Perhaps with one of my favorite pieces of dialogue from the 90's horror
film Jacob's Ladder:

Jezebel: Well, personally, I never went for church names.
Jezebel: What?
Jacob Singer: Where do you think Jezebel came from?
Jezebel: No one calls me that.
Jacob Singer: You're such a heathen, Jezzie. How'd I ever get involved with
such a fuckin' ninny?
Jezebel: You sold your soul, remember? That's what you told me.
Jacob Singer: Yeah? For what?
Jezebel: A good lay.
Jacob Singer: Look what I got.
Jezebel, Jacob Singer: The best.

Dialogue from Jacobs Ladder (1990's Psychological Horror Film)

Start at the beginning

I was lonely and destitute in Manchester, the place I had made my home
for several years. Drifting and living the roll and roll art lifestyle had
taken its toll., I thought I was the bee's knees. I was too proud of myself,
too arrogant, too away with the fairies to care about much of anyone
else of the world outside of my perfect dream bubble - floating away on
puffy pillows of maruijana to a single bed night by night, with just the
joyously confusing yet blissful lovemaking with Heri to distract me.

Heri and I met each other as lovers high in a jazz club, and as the tones
of incredible ambience poured from the speakers, she held my hand,
poor and battered as it was and simply smiled at me, with her eyes of
artistic wonder, she was beautifully queer. Queer in the way that all

queers are, defiantly strong and at one with her sexual nature, at peace with her bisexuality - to hell with the critics.

Strong like the way a wind is - blowing through the curtains. Heri was there for me at a time when I could not stop drifting, though it was certainly a confusing and short lived relationship, and only a relationship of sorts - 'friends on benefits'.

I will always remember the gulp of disappointment when she told me that last night didn't have to mean anything - then it all got a bit blurry from there as it can do.

Her ex used to be a man, now he was becoming a she. It was just one of those things you know. Really I am very ill at ease with those who shout and rave against trans people.

Yes it's a little odd at first, yes you may need to re-adjust a few ideas a bit. Best thing to do is talk to them, have a brew with them and you'll find out soon enough that they are no different from you and I. Is it really so much to ask to just let someone be themselves? I digress. We are all human which should always be the only thing that matters when it comes down to any questions of rights.

I was high most of the time and was unbeknowingly involved in a polyamourous joyride.

A few weeks of working together, arguing, quarreling and confusion followed. She was fantastic in bed. But she had chronic fatigue and depression and we were both such wandering violent souls so it was only a matter of time before we went our separate ways.

It ended on a sour note - it's risky mixing business with pleasure. I went to her screening, an eye opening film about 'dykes'. I was in alien territory as a beer chugging, plaid shirt wearing man with a bushy beard, but it was ok though I did think there was a disapproving glance perhaps when Heri kissed me on the cheek.

What's the point of bitterness though? It serves no one but your enemies.

My Enemies

- Bad taste
- Men who go on about their cocks all the time
- Women who bark on about the evils of homosexuality and the 'trans agenda'
- Chatting politics for too long
- Those who hate without thought
- Bad Ideas

To really hate something requires monumental effort, the type of effort that most sane and rational people realise is an utter waste of time. Personally I rarely take the time to hate my enemies or those that could be considered, I merely hold them in contempt.

Why bother when one can just lay back and watch them screw everything up themselves.
A cavalier attitude perhaps, but politics must sometimes be personal wherever you like it or not.

Marsha loves Oscar Wilde.

Marsha is not her real name, Marsha was my first real taste of love. She was the first woman who really understood me on a gut level that stung, the first woman I ever met and got to know in depth, swimming in her soul's waters. The only one with whom the tenacity and wildness of a wolf made I made love to, passionately. It was a long and more intense series of nights than anything I'd felt before - like magnets melting in a red orgy of flesh, a diabolical dance with the sapphire spirits in the mood of night.

We usually made love at night in the dark. I liked it that way as well though I was not used to it, not because I did not find her irresistible, but because it was moody, melodramatic and felt like an escape into some bohemian dreamworld. The first nickname I gave Marsha was minx, and that is exactly what she was to me, as I commanded her to kiss me, and made love to her for three days straight, three days of ecstatic hard fucking - primal.

My hands around her neck, and hers around mine, the thighs - like an angel from above, her ass hard and as bouncy as a peach sent from God itself.

She was not my first, I had lost my virginity 8 years ago for the first time, though I was much later than most - ripe enough age of 26, 10 years from when I now write this very memoir, still mentally wondering on the blistering snows and red leaves; Autumnal walks in the beating heart of Moscow.

My first fuck was my friends cousin at a local bar but enough of the sexual conquest talk, yes everyone knows men have sex, but what about something a bit deeper than sex? What about love?

What does that mean I hear you ask - Love? For me Love I think is a bond that can never break between two, making them one. It is a fixed point in time and space, but that is too literal a description. It is red, it is passion, it is knowledge, that is love - acceptance of our comings and goings, our entrances and exits, with long sighs, and holding each over under the covers.

Love can be a sigh as well as a screaming howl in the night. And so it was with Marsha. Almost the mother of my child. It's a long story. So let's tell it.

Online Dating

So I'd really rather rush through this part as I'm sure you dear reader do not want me to go on and on about my boasting (which is tiresome) and onto something serious, so first a note on online dating;

Long and short of it, like most sane people - I hate it. There you go; But with Marsha it was somehow different. Around that time I was generally having dates with disinterested women about the same age (34) who endured our dates. I would usually garble and ramble on about some obscure philosophy I was exploring or some bizarre musician I was getting into or my electronic music projects and writing adventures or banging on about philosophical ideas - Nietsche, Deleuze etc. Many women I find cannot really take the company of such a man of books and creative chaos as I can be. Many would make protests to the latter and there are an exceptional few who I could genuinely really communicate with, but many women are just simply not interested in living on the edge of the mind that way. Which is a shame, and I think something that will exponentially change in years to come.

Women love a bearded man progressing feminist talking points, but I've also learned its best to groom it now and again too. No woman can completely stand an old shaggy dog for company.

Around this time I was hanging around a lot with a physicist and she would mention how her tutors would sleep with female students in University. Personally I found that inoffensive but rather a depressing outlook on male and female relationships. How power dynamics disrupt the normal flow of love and make it something more cynical and perverse. I just imagined some pathetic man in glasses crying in his office, expecting his student to serve and massage his own ego, to convince him that he really did mean something in the grand scheme of things. The propensity for hubris from academics is occasionally incredible, holed up in their ivory towers waiting for blowjobs.

But I'm not a judgemental type so I'll decline judging too harshly. I can Imagine if I was in a position where I was teaching at adult level it might be quite tempting if one is single to have sex with an adult student, and really there isn't anything fundamentally wrong with it.

In some ways my own neurosis about sex is worse. I am a classical man who thinks about it a lot and can even drown in mastubatory excess at times, but actually doesn't have a great deal of it in reality, or has a lot with a significant partner with very very long dry patches in between. Simply put - I am genuinely monogamous.

Marsha messaged me one day from Moscow and I was shocked that someone from Russia was deciding to message me. Why would anyone bother to message me from so far abroad? It seemed so strange, I looked at her profile and found her looks interesting and intriguing but not immediately attractive. I had been making random video games and smoking weed for months, and enjoyed the life of the late millennial slacker, though it had started to get ugly.

She had a unique style which combined punk rock t-shirts, rock n' roll ripped jeans and indie thrift store chic. A cynical person might say she had the look of a 'manic pixie dream girl' - her hair was a brilliant green, would change colours every few months and she would sometimes sport a buzzcut - you get the idea. She seemed to combine a femininity with a certain strong masculine counterpoint in her nature, and I was to learn that she was indeed quite the ball kicker one might imagine, being as she was an political activist with aspirations to really change things in Russia for the better, a working class woman who had educated herself to the level of an expert in the English Language and linguistics and a genuinely bright and insightful caring soul who nursed others, even at times when she was having trouble nursing her own demons at times. She certainly nursed me as I returned home to my parents, after the seizure.

The Terror

I had bought what I assumed was normal weed from a guy on the street, which is always a bad idea. He offered me a discount on a bag for £15, five quid cheaper than the usual going rate in the area which usually was fixed to 20 or a '20 bag' as they call it on the streets.

Turns out it was 'Spice' - Spice is a terrible drug, it's a form of synthetic weed which has a synthetic form of THC in it and it was for a short time - completely legal. If you know anything about cannabis, it's THC which produces the high effect, but Synthetic THC is dangerous and often results in fits and temporary paralysis as the THC is a synthetic version of THC, with an unpredictable level of psychoactive potential. Cannabis is really quite harmless and the worst side effect is being a lazy arse and eating too much fast food, Spice is fucking not, it may as well be called 'devils weed speed'.

One might compare it in psychedelic terms with LSD and 'The Ladder' as described in the Horror film film Jacob's Ladder.

Chemist: We did it, most powerful thing I ever saw, even a bad trip and believe me I've had my share does not compare to the fury of the ladder'
Jacob : 'The Ladder?
Chemist: Yeh, that's what they called it, a fast trip straight down the ladder right to the primal fear, right to the base anger..'

And so it was for me. It was the 2nd time I tried the shit, and this time it was even worse than the first, I smoked the first drag and immediately knew something was wrong. I should've known from the smell, it smelt sharp and somehow wrong and the actual 'weed' was more like powder than weed, which if you know anything about is often clumpy and tough to the touch - as its often compressed depending on type, but this stuff was the consistency of solid powder.

After my first inhalation I froze in a stuttering motion like nude descending a staircase by Durchmap and fell down on my bed, as it felt like a giant wolf loomed over me, growling and darkness began to cloud my vision as I blacked out.

Blacking out is a terrifying experience and is something akin to a spiritual transcendence but it is a truly terrifying one. My eyes rolled back and I started screaming and howling with terror as a black cloud descended and all I could do was scream and thrash out as I lost control of my body, flailing around like a puppet possessed by a demon of violence.

The whole experience lasted about 10 mins I think, 10 mins of pure unbridled terror, and I after I was able to move around and returned back to the world of the living, I rang the ambulance who swiftly came to my tiny studio flat and escorted me to hospital for blood checks and a assessment. All I can say as always is thank you NHS for existing, for helping poor lost souls like I was who can fall through the cracks.

I did all this to myself, that was the worst part. It was not a high point, no pun intended.

Moscow Girl

Not long after my fit I decided I needed to take life slower, re-adapt to reality and really face what I was - a drug addict chained to his tobacco, weed, vape and stimulants, and so began the process of slow healing as I began to cut down on my intake, first stopping smoking weed slowly, and smoking less cigarettes. I was poor and destitute and relied on food banks for subsistence. I began to talk to Marsha more frequently and it was surreal as she would often talk to me doing some action or other - often environmental work or anti-corruption work.

She made me realize that if you have talents, it's best not to burn them up or yourself in the process of releasing them.
And for that I will always love her, even though we hurt one another.

www.ingramcontent.com/pod-product-compliance
Lightning Source LLC
Chambersburg PA
CBHW051318160726
47994CB00003B/1508